Ghostville Elementary®

No Haunting Zone!

Find out more spooky secrets about

Ghostville Elementary®

#1 *Ghost Class*
#2 *Ghost Game*
#3 *New Ghoul in School*
#4 *Happy Haunting!*
#5 *Stage Fright*
#6 *Happy Boo-Day to You!*
#7 *Hide-and-Spook*
#8 *Ghosts Be Gone!*
#9 *Beware of the Blabbermouth!*
#10 *Class Trip to the Haunted House*
#11 *The Treasure Haunt*
#12 *Frights! Camera! Action!*
#13 *Guys and Ghouls*
#14 *Frighting Like Cats and Dogs*
#15 *A Very Haunted Holiday*
#16 *Red, White, and BOO!*
#17 *No Haunting Zone!*

Ghostville Elementary®

No Haunting Zone!

by Marcia Thornton Jones
and
Debbie Dadey

illustrated by Guy Francis

A
LITTLE APPLE
PAPERBACK

SCHOLASTIC INC.
New York Toronto London Auckland Sydney
Mexico City New Delhi Hong Kong Buenos Aires

ISBN-13: 978-0-439-88365-8
ISBN-10: 0-439-88365-2

12 11 10 9 8 7 6 5 4 3 2 7 8 9 10 11 12/0

Printed in the U.S.A. 40
First printing, April 2007

To the best mom and dad ever, Thelma and Robert Thornton, for making sure our home was a NO HAUNTING ZONE!

—MTJ

To Mimi King

—DD

Contents

THE LEGEND

Sleepy Hollow Elementary School's Online Newspaper

This Just In: Community in Uproar!

Breaking News: The excitement of summer vacation just took a backseat to the wrecking ball parked outside Sleepy Hollow Elementary. The school board announced plans to tear down our school and replace it with a whiz-bang new building. Not everyone is happy about the news. Some people like our historic old building. The final decision is up in the air. One thing is certain: A new building would stop those rumors of Sleepy Hollow being haunted once and for all!

Stay tuned for more!

Your friendly fifth-grade reporter,
Justin Thyme

1
Summer

"Just a few more weeks," Nina said. She flipped her long black hair and shouted, "Then school will be out for the entire summer!"

Nina and her two best friends sat next to the monkey bars on the playground of Sleepy Hollow Elementary before school started.

"No more homework!" sang Cassidy.

"No more books!" Jeff chimed in.

"No more teachers' dirty looks!" Andrew screamed at the top of his lungs.

Andrew was not one of Nina's friends, but that didn't stop him from hanging upside down on the monkey bars above her. Andrew's baseball cap fell off his head and landed right in Nina's lap.

After Nina tossed Andrew's hat back up to him, she leaned close to her friends so Andrew couldn't hear. "I can't wait for summer," she whispered, "but I'm worried about the ghosts. What will they do while we're away?"

Nina, Cassidy, and Jeff glanced over at Sleepy Hollow Elementary. Everyone called it *Ghostville* Elementary because of the rumors that it was haunted. The three friends knew the rumors were true. They had seen the ghosts with their very own eyes. Even from the playground, Nina could see two of the ghosts, Sadie and Ozzy, inside their basement classroom. Their noses were pressed against the tiny dust-covered windows. Ozzy's nose was squished so flat it was as big and round as a pizza.

"The ghosts lived in our classroom for over one hundred years before we came along," Jeff said. "I'm sure they'll be fine for the summer."

School hadn't even started for the day,

and already the sun was hot and bright. Cassidy dropped her backpack onto the ground so she could pull her sweater off over her blond hair. "This will be the best summer ever. I'll get to use my brand-new computer program," she told Nina and Jeff. There was nothing Cassidy liked more than computers. She was so excited that she didn't care who was listening. "It's all about investing in the stock market. I'll learn how to become rich by the end of vacation."

Andrew flipped off the monkey bars and landed in a squat in front of Cassidy. He looked at her like she'd just blown Brussels sprouts out her nose. "You're kidding, right? You really think playing on a computer all summer will be fun?" Andrew sputtered.

"Of course," Cassidy said. "What else would I want to do?"

"Duh," Andrew said, slapping his forehead. "How about SOFTBALL?"

Cassidy's face grew as pale as the

clouds floating in the sky. It was no secret that Cassidy did not like sports. The last time she had swung a bat she tripped and fell in the dirt. “No, thanks,” she said. “I’ll stick to computer games.”

Andrew jammed his baseball cap down over his hair before grabbing his backpack. “We don’t want you on the team, anyway,” he said. Then he ran toward a group of kids on the sidewalk.

Nina, on the other hand, loved sports.

"I'm playing soccer this summer," she said.

"I'll film you practicing," Jeff said. "It'll make a good scene for my movie." Jeff planned to be a famous movie director when he grew up. He had decided to spend the summer making a movie called *Summer of the Kid-Eating Monsters.*

When they heard the bell ring, the three friends made their way around the building to the front doors. They were so excited talking about summer that they didn't notice the crowd of kids clustered in front of the building until they ran right into Andrew.

"What's going on?" Jeff asked. He shouldered past the twins, Carla and Darla, to get a better look.

Andrew pointed to the front doors of Ghostville Elementary. "You're never going to believe it!"

2
Closing!

A big yellow sign was plastered on the window. "A community meeting will be held," Jeff read aloud, "to discuss the closing of Sleepy Hollow Elementary School."

"Closing?" Cassidy asked.

"Closing," Nina said.

"Closing!" Andrew cheered. "Yay! They're closing school forever!" He threw his cap in the air and did a happy dance.

"But this is our school," Nina said. "They can't just shut it down."

Andrew stopped dancing long enough to thump Nina on the head. "Think, Brainless. Sleepy Hollow is over one hundred years old. We need a building that's new and shiny to replace this old dump."

Carla nodded. “It would be nice . . .”

“. . . to have a school that doesn’t leak,” her twin sister, Darla, finished.

“Or one that stays cool in the summer,” a girl named Barbara added.

“And warm in the winter,” a fourth grader chimed in.

Cassidy, Nina, and Jeff looked up at the old building. It was true that the paint was peeling, the roof was patched, and a few of the windows were cracked. Not

only that, there wasn't even enough room for all the students. That's why their third-grade class had been moved down to the basement. They were in the very classroom that had been boarded up for over one hundred years because of the rumors that it was haunted.

"Oh, no," Jeff muttered so only his friends could hear, "what will this mean for the ghosts?"

When Nina thought about a bulldozer leveling the only home the ghosts had known for so long, her stomach did a flip-flop. Unfortunately, the three kids were the only ones who even knew about the ghosts. The ghosts decided who could see and hear them, and, for some reason, they only let Nina, Cassidy, and Jeff know the room really *was* haunted.

Nina pushed to the front of the crowd and held up her hands to quiet them. "But . . . but . . . without the old school, our neighborhood just wouldn't seem the same," she stammered.

"So much history would be lost," Jeff added.

"They're right," Barbara said. "My father told me Sleepy Hollow is special because they don't build buildings like this anymore."

Carla nodded thoughtfully. "Instead of tearing it down . . ."

". . . they could always fix it up," Darla finished.

Other kids nodded. Everyone, that is, except Andrew. He was too busy doing his happy dance all the way into the building.

Nina frowned as she followed the rest of her class down the dusty steps to their basement classroom. Sadie knew something was wrong as soon as she saw Nina's face. Sadie knew about being sad. She was the saddest ghost in the basement. Maybe anywhere. She cried a lot. Her tears usually fell like water gushing from a fire hydrant. She hated seeing Nina looking so down in the dumps.

"What's wrong?" Sadie asked Nina.

Nina didn't want to be the one to break the news to the ghosts, so she kept her mouth shut. Besides, she didn't want any of the other kids in the class to see her talking to thin air.

"Don't be sad," Sadie begged. "Believe me, sad is no fun."

Sadie tried to cheer up Nina. The ghost puffed out her cheeks until her face was totally round. Then she changed colors so she looked like a giant smiley face.

The corners of Nina's mouth didn't even twitch.

Next, Sadie tickled Nina under her chin.

Nina shivered from the ghostly chill and pulled away.

"Something must be very wrong," Sadie said with a sniffle. "This calls for drastic action. Ghost action!"

3
Ghost Action

Pop!

Pop!

Two ghost boys appeared to help. Ozzy scrunched up his face, thinking hard. Nina knew that could only mean one thing. She had learned that ghosts had to concentrate to touch something in the real world. She shivered when his ghost fingers plucked a button right off of her sweater.

"Button? Button? Who has the button?" Ozzy asked. Nina sighed and pointed. "Oops," Ozzy said when he looked down and saw the button through his fingers. "How about this?" He sucked the button in through his lips.

The button ker-plopped into Ozzy's stomach where it tumbled like a Ping-

Pong ball in a clothes dryer. Nina groaned. Ozzy was definitely not cheering her up.

"Let me try," Nate said, shoving Ozzy aside. Ozzy flipped through the air and went straight through the bookshelf. His feet kicked and wiggled as he tried to free himself.

"Ever try skipping stones across a pond?" Nate asked.

Nina shook her head. "There's no pond," she whispered, making sure nobody else heard her.

"Never let a little detail get in your way," Nate told her. Then he concentrated very hard so he could pick up an eraser from Carla's desk. He tossed it across the room.

Boing! It bounced off Carla's desk.

Boing! It bounced on Darla's desk.

BOING! It landed right on Mr. Morton's head.

"What happened?" Mr. Morton said in surprise.

"Oops," Nate said, and he disappeared so fast he left a black hole.

Nina rested her head on her desk and sighed.

"Don't worry," Ozzy said, floating over to Nina's desk. "I'll have her grinning like a possum eating a yellow jacket."

Ozzy put his ghostly ear beside Nina's head. "How do skeletons get their mail?"

When Nina didn't move, Ozzy pretended to be riding a fast horse. "By the Bony Express!"

Nina groaned and Sadie moaned.

Sadie noticed that Cassidy and Jeff didn't look too happy, either. "Whatever is wrong," Sadie told Cassidy, "it must be very serious."

Before Cassidy could say a word, Mr. Morton clapped his hands. "Students,

I know you're all concerned about the notice."

"Notice?" Ozzy asked.

Carla raised her hand. "Mr. Morton, are they really going to tear down our school?"

"What?" Sadie and Becky screeched together before they both fainted on the floor. Ozzy took one look at Nina, then he disappeared with a loud crack that sounded like a window breaking.

Jeff thought he knew everything when it came to ghosts, but this was a new one for him. "Ghosts can faint?" Jeff whispered to Cassidy.

Cassidy shrugged. "I guess so."

"We don't know anything for sure," Mr. Morton said about the school closing. "It's all talk so far."

Cassidy tried to tell the ghosts that when they woke up, but they didn't listen. They hovered just above the floor and moaned all during reading and math.

To get anywhere, kids had to walk right through them. Of course, only Jeff, Cassidy, and Nina knew they were there.

"Brrrr," Andrew said when he stepped on Becky. Andrew's foot went through her stomach, but Andrew didn't even know it. "I can't wait for them to tear down this dump."

Andrew did his happy dance to the front of the room, not realizing the ruckus his words caused. Sadie rolled into a ball and moaned. Ozzy's fists turned into sledgehammers as he pounded the floor and shouted, "No! No! NOOOOOO!"

"We have to do something," Jeff said.

"What can we do?" Cassidy asked. "We're only kids."

"We should think of a way to save our school," Nina blurted, loud enough for other kids to hear.

Carla looked up from her social studies project. "We've been thinking," she said.

"And we have an idea," Darla said.

"What is it?" Nina asked.

Carla smiled. "You'll just have to wait . . ."

". . . and see," Darla said. Then she pretended to zip her lips and throw away the key.

4
Ghostly Tantrum

The next morning, Nina rang Cassidy's doorbell. Every day the girls walked to Jeff's house so they could all go to school together.

"Race you to Jeff's house," Nina told Cassidy.

"No!" Cassidy snapped. "I don't want to run, and I especially don't want to hit balls!"

Nina stopped on the sidewalk to look at her friend. "What are you talking about?"

"My grandfather signed me up for softball," Cassidy groaned. "He knows I hate getting sweaty. What was he thinking?"

"Sorry about that," Nina said. "But maybe you'll have fun."

"Swinging a piece of wood at a ball is

NOT my idea of fun," Cassidy said as Jeff tromped down the steps to join them.

"At least you'll be better off than the classroom ghosts," Nina pointed out. "They'll be dodging wrecking balls and bulldozers."

The three friends talked about the doomed school as they walked. On the playground, kids gathered to guess what their new building might look like. Carla and Darla sat on the steps, flipping through the pages of a fat library book. Nina, Jeff, and Cassidy decided to sneak into their classroom early to see the ghosts. They didn't see the ghosts, but they did see Olivia, the janitor.

Olivia had been the janitor at Sleepy Hollow for longer than anyone could remember. She always wore red overalls and earrings that jingled. Or maybe they jangled. She was known for taking care of animals that needed help. She helped any animal, no matter how ugly or prickly. Cassidy was surprised to see a normal-looking dog lying by Olivia's red sneakers.

"Have you heard the horrible news?" Olivia asked the kids with a sniff.

Jeff nodded. "It's not final, is it?"

Olivia usually smiled, but today she wore a frown. "I hope not. All those newfangled buttons and dials in modern buildings don't suit me. Sure, I have to work hard to keep that old boiler going throughout the year, but just think of the history in these bricks! Think of the architecture! Think of the people who have walked these halls. Why, I heard a President went to school here." Olivia's earrings jingled and jangled as she talked.

Cassidy tried to calm Olivia down by changing the subject. "Is this your new pet? He looks a little old."

Olivia looked at the dog by her feet and nodded. "Age doesn't mean a thing. Charlie is smart and can do a lot of tricks.

Old animals, people, and things have value, too, you know."

"There you are," said a mysterious voice.

Cassidy jumped. Jeff ducked. Nina shuddered when their principal, Ms. Finkle, appeared in the doorway and ran her long dagger-like fingernails through the hair on the old dog's head. "Olivia, I need you in the teachers' lounge. We must fix a problem before people use it as another reason to destroy our precious building."

Something about Ms. Finkle gave Nina the creeps. Maybe it was her blood-red lipstick. It could've been Ms. Finkle's milky-white skin. Or maybe it was the way she eyed kids as if they were a midnight snack.

Charlie barked and stood up on his hind legs. Cassidy laughed when the dog did a little dance.

"This is a perfectly good school," Ms. Finkle said as they walked away.

"It's an outrage to tear it down. Wasteful, that's what it is," Olivia told her.

Ms. Finkle put her hand on Olivia's shoulder. "This building is our home," she told Olivia. "What would we do without it?"

"*Woof,*" said Charlie.

"Wow," Jeff said after they'd left. "Why are Olivia and Ms. Finkle so mad? Shouldn't they want a new school?"

"They're as upset as the ghosts," Nina said.

Cassidy's face grew so pale it made her freckles stand out. She grabbed Nina's arm. "Ms. Finkle did say this old building was her home. And she and Olivia have been here longer than anyone can remember. You don't suppose they're ghosts, too, do you?"

"You're crazy," Jeff told her.

Nina frowned. "It just doesn't seem right to tear the school down around our ghosts. What will happen to them?"

"Maybe the twins can help," Jeff said.

Carla and Darla came into the classroom loaded with old books. They stuck their noses in two big books and started reading without saying a word.

"They're no help at all," Cassidy said.

"Oh, no," Nina said as green glittered in the middle of the room. "Here we go again." Ozzy, Becky, and Sadie appeared in a green glow and fell on the floor moaning.

Ozzy didn't just moan, he wailed. Jeff put his hands over his ears to block out the horrible noise. Becky kicked the floor like a spoiled two-year-old in a candy store. Sadie cried and made a puddle of tears.

Cassidy sighed. "We're in the middle of another ghost tantrum."

5
Town Meeting

The gymnasium was crowded that night. People from all over the neighborhood came to hear the plans. Nina, Jeff, and Cassidy huddled in the back of the room while their parents sat in seats up front. Even Cassidy's grandfather and Nina's grandmother had come.

Men and women in suits sat at a long table in front of the room. Ms. Finkle sat in the middle, quietly staring at each of the board members. Olivia hovered in the shadows, but Cassidy noticed the glint of light sparkling off Olivia's earrings.

"A new school will put Sleepy Hollow on the cutting edge of education," a man in a suit said.

"We already are the best," Ms. Finkle interrupted. "We have the best teachers.

The best materials. The best students. A building won't make us better."

"A new building will add grace and beauty to the neighborhood," the man argued.

"New will look out of place next to the old houses here," a lady pointed out.

"But new is nice!" the man sputtered.

The crowd fell silent as a mixture of moaning voices echoed throughout the gym. "No! No! NOOOOOOOOOOO!"

The three best friends knew exactly what they were hearing. Ghost voices.

Nina ducked. Cassidy gasped. Jeff jumped up and turned in a complete circle, "Where are they?" Jeff asked as he searched the room.

"How could they escape the basement?" Nina whimpered.

Cassidy waited for the ghostly voices to moan again as the rest of the crowd began to murmur.

"NOOOOOOOOOOO!" came the haunting chorus again.

“There,” Cassidy pointed to the heating radiator. “They’re sending their voices through the pipes,” she whispered to her friends. One of the men at the head table pounded the gavel to get everyone’s attention.

“That,” the man announced, “is proof that we need a new school. Everything in this building is old. Old pipes. Old heating system. Old, old, OLD!”

“There is nothing wrong with old,” said a man in the front, and a group of people cheered.

“Who said that?” Nina asked.

Cassidy knew. She recognized the voice. It was her grandfather.

“He’s right,” Ms. Finkle agreed. “We must preserve our history.”

After that there was lots of shouting and arguing until the man running the meeting pounded a gavel on the table.

“This meeting is adjourned,” he said. “We will come back on Thursday to discuss the new school.”

"Maybe the neighbors changed the school board members' minds," Cassidy said as they walked home.

"I hope so," Nina said.

But the next day at school, a huge crane with a wrecking ball sat outside the building. Carla and Darla, each clutching a stack of books, stared at it.

"Yee-haw!" Andrew yelled when he walked up behind Nina, Cassidy, and Jeff. "They're going to knock this old building down."

Nina felt sick to her stomach.

Later that day, when Nina went out in the hallway to get a drink, she saw Sadie huddled in a corner and felt even worse.

Sadie's hair hung in limp strands across her face. Her skin had faded to the color of creamed peas. Huge tears dribbled down her cheeks and dripped to the floor.

"Don't cry," Nina said, squatting so close that the ghost's breath made Nina's teeth chatter.

"You don't understand," Sadie told Nina. "If they tear our home down, where will we go? What will we do?"

"Can't you stay in the new building?" Nina asked.

Sadie shook her head. "I don't think so. This is all we have left of what we once had. How can we go where there's nothing but newness?"

Sadie sobbed so hard she melted into a pool of tears.

6
Think. Think. THINK!

Later that afternoon, Jeff and Nina watched Cassidy practice with her new softball team.

When Cassidy played left field, she dropped the ball. At third base, she tripped instead of tagging out the runner. Even worse, Cassidy fell down every time she swung the bat.

"I have to admit," Jeff said, "Cassidy stinks."

"Shh," Nina said. "She'll hear you."

"Don't worry," Cassidy said, coming up beside them. "I already know I'm bad."

"Maybe I can help," Nina suggested.

"We can give you some pointers at my house," Jeff added.

Cassidy shook her head. "I'm too old to learn this game."

"Of course you're not," Nina said. "You sound as bad as Sadie."

"What's that supposed to mean?" Cassidy asked as the three friends left the ball field and headed to Jeff's house.

Nina explained what Sadie had told her. Nina finished by saying, "Sadie acted like the ghosts don't want to change."

"Maybe they *can't* change," Jeff said.

"What do you mean, *can't*?" Cassidy asked as the three friends stepped into Jeff's backyard. Balls, bikes, and bats were scattered on the patchy lawn. Nina snatched a bat off the grass and swung it through the air with perfect form, but Cassidy wasn't watching.

"Remember what happened when Sadie crashed Nina's birthday party?" Jeff asked.

Sadie had popped up at Nina's house, far from the school. By the end of the night, Sadie had faded to a mere glimmer. It was a close call, but they managed to get her back to Ghostville Elementary before she faded completely.

"The only reason she was able to leave the school at all was because Nina wore Sadie's necklace," Jeff continued.

"And Ozzy could only get out of the basement when he took a sliver of wood that belonged to his desk," Nina said slowly.

Cassidy broke out in a sweat. "You're right," she said. "Ghosts have to stay with their belongings. That's why they can't leave the school basement."

"So if they tear down Sleepy Hollow Elementary," Nina said, "the very belongings that keep the ghosts there will be scattered all over town."

"And so will the ghosts!" Cassidy shrieked.

"That can only mean one thing," Jeff said. "If we don't think of a way to save our school, then all of Sleepy Hollow will be haunted by some very unhappy ghosts."

"And the ghosts will be separated forever," Cassidy said. "We can't let that happen. The ghosts would be so sad."

"What can we do?" Nina asked. "We're only kids."

Cassidy grabbed the bat from Nina. "Remember what Olivia said about her old dog, Charlie? She said that age doesn't mean a thing. She's right. It

doesn't matter how old we are. It only matters that we're doing the right thing." Cassidy swung the bat hard through the air, and this time she didn't fall down.

Nina clapped. Jeff cheered.

"Think. Think. THINK!" Nina said. "How can we save our school?"

"We could make signs and march in a demonstration," Cassidy suggested.

Jeff shook his head. "That wouldn't stop them."

"We could chain ourselves to the front doors so they can't tear it down," Nina said.

Jeff shook his head again. "You know our parents would ground us for life if we got between a wrecking ball and the school."

"Then you come up with something," Cassidy said, pointing the bat at Jeff.

Suddenly, Jeff smiled. "I have the perfect plan," he said.

7
The Perfect Plan

The next afternoon, Cassidy, Jeff, and Nina waited for everyone to leave their basement classroom at the end of the day. Carla and Darla took forever. Their stack of books was so big, they could barely see over the top.

"This just might work," Cassidy said as Jeff put a DVD in his video camera.

"If I don't itch to death first," Nina complained, scratching under the collar of her old-fashioned costume. When the kids had told Mr. Morton about their idea to make a movie about Sleepy Hollow's history to show at the second school board meeting, he had agreed to let them stay after school to film it. They had to ignore the sound of workers tromping down the halls, taking measurements and notes.

"It'll be worth it," Jeff told his friends. "You know what they say, a picture is worth a thousand words. This DVD will be a snapshot of history."

"Okay," Cassidy said to Nina. "You be the student, and I'll be the teacher."

"Why can't I be the teacher?" Nina asked.

Cassidy sighed, but before she could answer, green sparkles filled the air near Nina's head. Sadie appeared right above Nina's black braids. "What are you doing?" Sadie moaned.

More green shimmered beside Cassidy. "Oooh," cried Becky. "I like your dresses." Becky and Sadie concentrated so that they could touch the long skirts that Nina and Cassidy wore. Every ghostly touch sent cold chills through the girls.

"We're filming a movie to save the school," Nina told the ghosts.

"Oooooh, thank you," Sadie moaned. She forgot that she was a ghost and tried to hug Nina, but Sadie ended up falling through Nina's body. Nina shivered.

Becky said, "We'll help."

"No, no," Jeff said. He pointed to a corner of the room. "Just float over there, out of the way."

Sadie and Becky flew over to the corner to watch. Cassidy was surprised. Since ghosts could do whatever they wanted, they usually didn't want to do what the kids asked.

"Action!" Jeff yelled.

"Nina?" Cassidy said, pretending to be an old-fashioned teacher. "Please tell us about Sleepy Hollow School."

Nina folded her hands in front of her and said, "The original Sleepy Hollow Elementary was built in 1845 by local parents. They . . ."

Sadie hopped in front of Nina. "Tell them my granddaddy hauled the logs to build it." Sadie rolled around Nina as if she were a big wooden log.

Becky jumped on the Sadie log and danced. "Tell them my Uncle Bill Jessup drove the first teacher all the way through unsettled territory. They were almost killed by bandits." Becky pretended to be a wagon driver and zipped around the room. She went straight through desks, chairs, and even bookshelves.

"Stop!" Jeff yelled. "I'm making this movie."

Becky shook her head at Jeff and said, "Boys. They think they know everything."

Sadie giggled. "But they don't know what we're going to do next." Sadie soared over to Becky and whispered in her ear. Then the two ghosts disappeared faster than flies in winter.

8
Doomed

"Ahhhhh!"

"Ahhhhh!"

Two grown men screamed from out in the hallway.

Jeff stopped filming.

Cassidy dropped a piece of chalk, and it shattered on the floor.

Nina pulled an old-fashioned shawl up over her head.

All three hurried to the door to see what was happening.

The men huddled at the far end of the hall. One of them pulled at his collar and gasped. The other had rolled into a ball on the floor.

"What's wrong with them?" Nina whispered.

"We have to go see," Cassidy said.

"No, we don't," Jeff said, but he followed as Cassidy led the way.

Step-by-step, the three kids crept along the basement hallway, their backs pressed against the damp bricks. Cassidy sniffed. "What is that smell?" she asked.

Nina and Jeff tested the air. "Smells like burning hair," Jeff said.

Nina shook her head. "I think it smells like rotten hamburger."

"Make it stop!" one of the men whimpered.

"Go away," hollered the other one.

"What are they talking about?" Nina asked.

Jeff pulled on Cassidy's sleeve. "There," he said. "That's the problem."

Sadie and Becky were nothing more than a transparent breeze, but they were a lot scarier than wind. The two ghost girls had joined forces and were using ghost power to trap the men in the corner.

Green blobs oozed from the ghosts'

noses. As the ghost-goo dripped, the ghost girls caught it and rolled it into balls. The balls Sadie made turned to frost. Becky's blob-balls steamed like they had been cooked in a campfire. They threw their ghostly blobs at the construction workers. The men couldn't see them, but they felt them. One of the men had sweat pouring down his face. The other shivered as if he were in a freezer.

"Leave us alone!" the ghost girls chanted with each round of goop they threw.

"D . . . d . . . did you hear something?" one of the men asked the other.

The second man gulped. He nodded. "The stories are true," he yelped. "This place is haunted."

"Let's get out of here!" the first man said.

The skinny man yelled and ran for his life, straight through Sadie. He rushed out of the basement, covered with green

goo. The second man was hot on his heels.

"What are you doing?" Jeff asked Becky once the men had thundered up the steps.

Sadie fluttered toward the kids, dripping green goo. "We were just using a little ghost power to scare them away."

"No, no, no!" Cassidy told the ghosts. "Ghost power won't work. If they really think this place is haunted, it will give them all the more reason to tear it down."

Nina explained what had happened at the meeting when the ghosts sent their voices through the pipes. "The school board only used it as another reason to build a brand-new school," she finished.

Sadie and Becky turned the color of rotten spinach. "Do you really think so?" Becky whispered.

Jeff nodded. "That's why our movie is so important. We have to prove how special this old building is."

"From now on, this is a no haunting zone," Nina said. "Promise."

"Ghosts shouldn't make promises," Becky said, "because a promise lasts forever."

"And forever is a long time," added Sadie.

And then they both popped out of sight, leaving nothing more than a faint, green goo stain on the floor.

9
Smithereens

Jeff, Nina, and Cassidy stayed until dinner time to finish the video. Every once in a while, they felt the cold draft of a ghost watching over their shoulders. Even though the ghosts made no promises, they left the three kids alone. Still, they were a distraction, and Jeff couldn't get the scenes he wanted.

They decided to work on the project at Cassidy's house. Then Jeff stayed up late to finish. The next morning, his eyes had dark circles under them when he stood up in front of the class to show the completed video.

"Roll 'em," Jeff directed.

He popped his DVD in and hit play. Mr. Morton and the rest of the third grade settled in to watch. THE STORY OF SLEEPY

HOLLOW flashed across the screen. A green ghost cloud wiggled and squirmed beside the television. It grew thicker. Sadie, Ozzy, and Becky appeared, seen only by Nina, Cassidy, and Jeff.

"They remembered my granddaddy!" Sadie screeched as the video played. For once she wasn't sad. Her skin turned a bright shade of lavender as she watched.

Cassidy had to admit her own grandfather did an excellent job of acting out the part. He had been happy to help them and had even come up with the idea of piling baseball bats like logs on an old-fashioned sled. Then he dressed in overalls and a straw hat, pretending to drag the heavy load across Cassidy's backyard while Jeff recorded the scene.

Cassidy's grandfather also helped the kids turn a picnic table into a covered wagon. Cassidy and Nina were the bandits, and Nina's *abuela* made a very convincing school marm. Nina smiled when Becky cheered.

Jeff's film followed the history of the school all the way up to the present day. "Our school must be saved," Jeff's voice boomed from the speakers. "It is a part of Sleepy Hollow's yesterdays, todays . . . and tomorrows!"

THE END flashed across the screen in big letters.

Ozzy grabbed Becky's arm and do-si-doed her across the room, not even noticing when they danced through Mr. Morton's desk and file cabinet. Sadie turned somersaults. The third grade broke into cheers. Mr. Morton clapped. Carla and Darla even gave them a standing ovation. Everyone was impressed. Everyone, that is, except Andrew. He crossed his arms and slumped in his seat.

"Our plan is to show this at the board meeting tonight," Jeff announced. "When the school board understands how

valuable our building is, they'll have no choice but to stop the demolition!"

Mr. Morton wiped away chalk dust from his glasses. "Excellent idea," he said.

"No, it isn't," Andrew said. "It's stupid, stupid, stupid. Nobody cares about what happened a long time ago, and neither should we."

"You're wrong," Carla said.

"People care," added Darla. She held up one of the history books she had checked out from the library as proof.

Then a group of boys started a chant. "Yay, Jeff! Yay, Jeff!" Soon, everyone else joined in. "Jeff! Jeff! Jeff!"

Jeff took the DVD from the player. He bowed to the class as he headed back to his desk. He was so busy bowing that he didn't see Andrew's foot sticking out in the aisle until it was too late.

Wham!

Jeff landed flat on his face. The DVD rolled out of his hands.

Crunch!

Andrew's foot smashed it to smithereens.

"You did that on purpose," Cassidy told Andrew. Nina helped Jeff off the floor.

"That's okay," Nina said. "Jeff can just bring a copy to the meeting tonight."

Jeff looked at the slivers of his movie on the floor.

"Copy?" he squeaked.

10
New Tricks

Jeff sat on the bleachers during Cassidy's game, his head in his hands. "I can't believe I forgot to make a copy," he moaned. "All directors know to backup their masterpieces."

Nina sat next to Jeff and patted him on the back. They had been sitting on the bleachers for an hour while Cassidy practiced with her softball team. So far, Jeff had said the same thing two hundred and ninety-three times. Nina knew. She had counted.

"They're going to tear down the school, and it's all my fault," Jeff groaned. "The ghosts will never forgive me."

"It isn't your fault," Nina said. "It's Andrew's."

Just then Andrew swung the bat and hit a foul over third base. His next swing hit nothing but air. Nina knew it wasn't good sportsmanship, but she clapped when Andrew struck out.

"Look, Jeff," Nina said. "It's Cassidy's turn. Sit up and watch."

Jeff sighed and lifted his head from his hands. So far Cassidy had struck out a total of four times, but at least she hadn't fallen down.

"Keep your eye on the ball," Nina hollered.

The pitcher wound up and then let the ball fly.

Swoosh! Cassidy swung the bat so hard she turned in a complete circle, but she stayed on her feet.

"Strike one!" shouted the umpire.

"Square your shoulders," Nina called.

The pitcher eyed Cassidy. Then he nodded and let loose a fastball.

Swoosh! Cassidy swung again.

"Strike two!" shouted the umpire.

"Wait for the ball to come to you!" Jeff yelled.

Cassidy heard her friends. She lifted the bat. She eyed the ball.

The pitcher hurled the ball through the air.

Cassidy waited. And waited. And waited. Finally, when the ball neared home plate, she swung.

Smack! The bat connected and the ball soared past second base.

Nina and Jeff cheered as Cassidy ran the bases. First. Second. Third. All the way to home plate.

The team surrounded Cassidy. Nina and Jeff rushed through the crowd to their friend.

"You did it!" Nina laughed. "You really did it!"

Cassidy grinned. "I guess it's true. You *can* teach an old dog new tricks!"

Nina stopped cheering. "That's it!" Nina yelled. "That's the answer. I know how to save the school!"

11
Old Dog

"What is she going to do?" Jeff asked Cassidy as they made their way to the second school board meeting. All around the school, adults and children held signs. Some said SAVE OUR SCHOOL while others said BUILDING THE FUTURE. Everyone seemed to be shouting at one another.

Cassidy shrugged and followed Nina into the building. This time, Nina didn't stay in the back, but squeezed past the crowd up to the front. Cassidy and Jeff sat beside her on the floor.

The same people from the last meeting sat around the big table in front. Ms. Finkle was in the middle of them all. Nina thought she saw Olivia dart behind a curtain.

A gavel slammed down on a table, and the meeting started.

"We'll begin with those who have signed up to speak." A man in a suit paused to look at a list. "First up is a Miss Nina Martinez."

Cassidy and Jeff gasped as Nina stood up and walked to the front of the gym. Nina looked very small standing behind the tall microphone. She stood on her

tiptoes to talk. “Everyone has been fighting about tearing down the school,” Nina said softly.

She cleared her throat and looked at the crowd. Hundreds of eyes stared back at her. Only a few of them looked friendly. Ms. Finkle frowned at her, but Nina gulped and continued, “I am here to propose that we can have it both ways. We can teach our old school new tricks.”

“What’s that girl talking about?” a man in the back called out.

“Make her sit down!” a lady yelled. “She’s just a kid. What does she know?”

“I am a kid,” Nina said bravely. “And this is my school. I say we can make it modern and still preserve our history. Let’s fix up the old school and add on a new part.”

A murmur went through the crowd until the man in the suit slammed the gavel down again. “Thank you, Miss Martinez,” said the man. “We’ve already looked into remodeling and found it

would be too expensive. It's actually cheaper to tear the school down."

Nina hung her head as she left the stage and sat down. The next speakers were a blur. She couldn't stop thinking about the ghosts. What would happen to them? Would they disappear forever in the construction dust?

Finally, the man with the gavel announced the last speakers. "We have Carla and Darla Welch."

Nina, Jeff, and Cassidy looked up in surprise. What were the twins going to do?

Carla and Darla set up a computer and dimmed the lights. They showed pictures from the first Sleepy Hollow building. Then they showed pictures of a President, a scientist, and an astronaut.

Carla began talking, "Ladies and gentlemen, we have done . . ."

". . . a lot of research on Sleepy Hollow Elementary," Darla continued. "We found out that many famous people went to school here."

A murmur of surprise went around the gymnasium as Carla took over. "We talked to the people who run the National Trust for Historic Preservation. They want to make Sleepy Hollow Elementary an official historic site and maybe even help pay to fix it up."

This time, the crowd roared with excitement, and Darla had to shout into the microphone. "It is illegal to tear down a historic site, so Sleepy Hollow must be preserved."

The man in the suit slammed the gavel down hard to regain order. "Ladies and gentlemen, we will dismiss this meeting to give the school board time to study these new findings. As of now, the demolition has been officially halted."

The crowd stood up and clapped and cheered.

Cassidy saw Olivia dart out from behind the curtains to give Ms. Finkle a high-five.

There was so much noise that Nina was

pretty sure nobody noticed when ghostly cheers erupted from the heating pipes.

Nina hugged Carla and Darla. "You saved our school," Nina told the twins. "Thanks."

"We should thank you," Carla said.

"Why me?" Nina asked.

Carla explained, "Because you were the only one brave enough to speak up about the value of our school when you first saw the notice. It made us . . ."

". . . think about it in a different way," Darla finished.

Nina smiled. She knew that her school was old. She knew it needed fixing. But she also knew it had something that no other school had. Not only did it have great kids, it also came complete with ghosts. And those ghosts still had a place to live . . . Ghostville Elementary.

All it took was a little bit of ghost power . . . and a whole lot of kid power.

About the Authors

Marcia Thornton Jones and Debbie Dadey got into the *spirit* of writing when they worked together at the same school in Lexington, Kentucky. Debbie currently *haunts* Ft. Collins, CO, with her three children, three dogs, and husband. Marcia remains in Lexington, KY, where she lives with her husband and two cats.

Debbie and Marcia have fun with other spooky stories like The Adventures of the Bailey School Kids and The Bailey School Kids Jr. Chapter Book series. Debbie also writes the Swamp Monster in the Third Grade series as well as some single titles like her upcoming book, *The Worst Name in Third Grade*. Marcia's middle-grade novel, *Champ*, is available now. Learn more at www.BaileyKids.com.